KT-572-468

Aisha
the Astronaut
Fairy

By Daisy Meadows

ORCHARD

www.rainbowmagicbooks.co.uk

CUMBRIA LIBRARIES

3 8003 04859 7520

Aisha
The Astronaut
Fairy

Rainbow Magic Reading Challenge!

Read the story and collect your fairy points to climb the Reading Rainbow at the back of the book.

This book is worth 5 points.

To Bella and Pippa

Special thanks to
Rachel Elliot

First published in Great Britain in 2019 by The Watts Publishing Group

1 3 5 7 9 10 8 6 4 2

© 2019 Rainbow Magic Limited.
© 2019 HIT Entertainment Limited.
Illustrations © Orchard Books 2019

HiT entertainment

The moral rights of the author and illustrator have been asserted.
All characters and events in this publication, other than those clearly in the public domain,
are fictitious and any resemblance to real persons, living or dead, is purely coincidental.

All rights reserved.
No part of this publication may be reproduced, stored in a retrieval system, or transmitted, in any
form or by any means, without the prior permission in writing of the publisher, nor be otherwise
circulated in any form of binding or cover other than that in which it is published and without a
similar condition including this condition being imposed on the subsequent purchaser.

A CIP catalogue record for this book is available from the British Library.

ISBN 978 1 40835 512 1

Printed and bound in Great Britain by CPI Group (UK) Ltd, Croydon, CR0 4YY

The paper and board used in this book are made from wood from responsible sources

Orchard Books
An imprint of Hachette Children's Group
Part of The Watts Publishing Group Limited
Carmelite House, 50 Victoria Embankment, London EC4Y 0DZ

An Hachette UK Company
www.hachette.co.uk
www.hachettechildrens.co.uk

Jack Frost's Spell

Those brainy fairies make me cross.
One day Jack Frost will be their boss.
I'll solve each baffling mystery
And make each great discovery.

I'll steal their magic books away
And grow more crafty every day.
No clever-clogs in history
Will be as brilliant as me!

Contents

Chapter One
Sleepover in the City

"This is going to be such a cool sleepover," said Kirsty Tate.

She shared a smile with her best friend, Rachel Walker. They were standing at the top of the Science Museum steps, hugging their pillows.

"I wonder if Selena the Sleepover Fairy will be watching over us," said Rachel.

Kirsty felt a rush of excitement. The girls had been friends with the fairies ever since they had met on Rainspell Island.

"I hope so," she said. "Do you remember our adventure with her at the National Museum sleepover?"

"Of course," said Rachel, laughing. "How could I forget spooky stories in the crypt and goblins running wild in the museum?"

Just then, a group of children walked past, and the girls quickly changed the subject. They had promised the queen of Fairyland never to tell their incredible secret to anyone else.

"Night-time seems different in the city," said Rachel.

"Yes," said Kirsty with a laugh.

"It's very different from night-time in Wetherbury."

Her home village was so quiet at night that even one vehicle would shatter the peace. Here, the whizzing traffic made a constant hum. Although it was dark, the streets were glowing. Neon theatre signs, bright streetlights, dazzling shop displays and sweeping car headlights lit up every brick and paving stone.

"I know the stars are up there," said Rachel, gazing into the night sky. "The city's just too well-lit to see them. Even the moon doesn't seem quite as bright."

"It feels a bit odd to be here in our pyjamas," said Kirsty. "At least we're not the only ones."

The square below the museum was filled with children, all dressed in their pyjamas and also clutching pillows. The

science museum was holding one of its famous sleepovers, and crowds of school groups, families and clubs were heading towards the main entrance.

"This is going to be the most exciting night of my life," said a little boy as he skipped past Rachel and Kirsty.

"It makes me feel all fizzy inside to see everyone so happy," said Kirsty.

"Fizzy inside?" said Mr Tate, walking up behind them. "That doesn't sound like a recipe for a good night's sleep."

Kirsty giggled and gave her dad a hug.

"Tonight isn't about sleeping," she said. "It's about having fun!"

Mr Tate ruffled her hair and laughed.

"Let's go in and find out where to put our sleeping bags," he said.

They joined the people who were

crowding in through the main entrance. Inside, museum staff were checking people's names on tablets and making sure that everyone was on the list. Mr Tate went up to a young man and gave him their names.

"Welcome to the Science Museum," said the young man. "You'll be sleeping in our Discover Space gallery, next to the planetarium. Please find a place to set up your camp and then head into the planetarium for our show."

Tingling with excitement, the girls and Mr Tate followed the signs to the Discover Space gallery. It was a large room with walls of dark blue. Models of planets hung from high beams. Everything was lit in shades of blue and purple, and tiny silver lights twinkled in

the ceiling like distant stars. Rachel and
Kirsty rolled out their sleeping bags and
then hurried through a large wooden
door into the planetarium, followed by
Mr Tate.

It was so dark that the girls couldn't see their own feet. Then they saw a woman wearing the science museum uniform with a small head torch attached to her hat.

"Welcome to the planetarium," she said. "I'm Grace. Did you know that the light from the stars takes millions of years to reach Earth? When you look at them, you are looking back in time."

She pointed up at the great, domed ceiling. It was glittering with stars.

"Is that the real sky?" asked Rachel with a gasp.

"It's a film," said Grace, smiling. "The walls, the ceiling and even the floor are all a gigantic screen. Take a seat and get ready for a journey into space."

Chapter Two
A Magical Surprise

"Oh my goodness," said Kirsty, leaning back in her padded chair and looking up. "This is incredible."

On the screen, stars and planets whooshed past in the blink of an eye.

"It feels as if we're really up there," Rachel said.

"This is the closest I'll ever get to being an astronaut," said Mr Tate with a chuckle.

The seats filled up as more people arrived, gasping in wonder. At last the big door closed, and a deep rumble of music stopped everyone talking. There was an expectant silence. Then a voice thundered around them.

"Welcome to the science museum!"

The crowd cheered and clapped.

"Your first activity of the night is a trip into outer space," the voice went on. "Look out for black holes as we hitch a ride to the International Space Station."

A large spacecraft appeared above them. Rachel and Kirsty held on to the arms of their chairs.

"It really feels as if we're whizzing

around the space station," said Kirsty.
"I'm getting dizzy."

"And I'm getting travel sick," said Mr
Tate sadly. "I'm sorry, girls, but I'll have
to miss out on this trip. Will you be OK if
I wait for you back at our camp?"

"Of course," the girls replied.

Mr Tate left as the deep voice boomed
on.

"The International Space Station is a

place where astronauts live when they're in space. It orbits around Earth, but it's not just a home. It's a science lab too. Astronauts from all over the world work together to learn more about space."

The screen changed as they zoomed inside the space station. The girls saw lots of complicated equipment, and men and women floating in the air.

"The space station is made of many pieces called modules. It's as big as a house inside! Solar panels collect energy from the sun and turn it into electricity. There's a big window and there are doors called airlocks. Astronauts can even go outside for space walks."

As the voice went on explaining about the work of the space station, Rachel felt Kirsty tugging at her sleeve.

"Look under the seat in front of you," Kirsty whispered.

Something was glowing in the darkness.

"Is it part of the show?" Rachel asked.

"It's even more exciting than the show," said Kirsty. "I think it's magic!"

Together, the best friends bent down to peer under the seat, and then smiled.

A tiny fairy was standing there with her finger to her lips. In the darkness, the tip of her tiny wand had a silvery glow.

"Hello, Rachel and Kirsty," the little fairy whispered. "I'm Aisha the Astronaut Fairy, and I need your help."

The girls exchanged a glance. They were always ready to help the fairies, but it would be tricky inside the planetarium.

"Hide under my hair," said Rachel. "We can creep out while everyone's listening to the show. It's lucky that we're

at the end of the row."

It was so dark that no one noticed them tiptoeing towards the door. They slipped out into the Discover Space gallery and then into the corridor. There was no one around.

"Everyone's listening to the show," said Kirsty. "It's safe, Aisha."

The little fairy flew out from beneath

Rachel's hair. She was wearing a silvery purple dress with silver space boots, and her dark hair was tied up in a loose bun. She looked worried.

"I desperately need your help," she said, fluttering in front of the girls. "I'm one of the Discovery Fairies. It's my job to look after astronauts as they explore and make new discoveries. This morning, something terrible happened. Please, will you come to Fairyland with me?"

"Of course," said the girls at once.

Aisha raised her wand, and instantly sparkling stars surrounded Rachel and Kirsty. They felt their gossamer fairy wings quivering, and they rose off the ground. The stars dazzled them. Then, suddenly, they were no longer inside the museum. They were flying towards

a domed glass building beside a launch
pad. A silver rocket was standing on the
launch pad. Around the dome, the grass
was dotted with amazing sculptures.

Each one was formed from complicated geometric shapes and patterns.

"What a cool-looking place," said Kirsty.

"This is where we watch over all the discoveries that are made in the human world," said Aisha. "Come and meet the other Discovery Fairies."

She swooped down towards the glass dome. As she got closer, a panel slid open in the glass. Aisha flew in, followed by Rachel and Kirsty.

"Welcome to Mission Control," said Aisha.

Chapter Three
Book Burglars

Rachel and Kirsty were inside a
large room filled with computers and
complicated panels. Everything was
still and quiet. Three fairies were sitting
gloomily in the middle of the room. They
looked up when they saw Rachel and
Kirsty.

"This is Orla the Inventor Fairy, Annie the Detective Fairy and Elsie the Engineer Fairy," said Aisha.

"We're so happy you've come," said Annie, fluttering forward. "You're our only hope."

"We're so glad to meet you all," said
Kirsty.

"Let me show you what happened
this morning," said Orla. "I've invented
a Seeing Screen so you can see for
yourselves."

She tapped a nearby desk, and a large
screen rose up. It showed a picture of
Mission Control, but it looked very
different. The four fairies were flitting
between panels of levers, computer
screens and glowing buttons.

"This morning we were so busy that we
didn't notice when someone came into
the lab," said Aisha, pointing to a door
that was opening behind the fairies. "We
get lots of visitors and they're always
welcome. So we didn't even turn around
until it was too late."

A long, thin nose poked through the
door, followed by a sharp chin and spiky
hair.

"Jack Frost," said Rachel. "Uh-oh."

The Ice Lord crept in, with four
sniggering goblins behind him. He slipped
through a doorway on the other side of
the lab.

"That's the way to the Discovery Library," said Aisha.

Inside, the curved walls were lined with books. Jack Frost stood in the middle of the library and looked around, curling his lip.

"Find those books," he hissed. "Now!"

The goblins scampered around the library, pulling books down and scattering them over the floor. Then Jack Frost pointed at four colourful books that were standing alone on the highest shelf.

"Mine," he whispered.

The goblins clambered up the shelves
as if they were climbing a ladder.
Squawking with victory, they each took
one of the books and scrambled down.

"Ha ha!" Jack Frost shouted.

Just then, the four Discovery Fairies
appeared in the doorway of the library.
The goblins ran to hide behind Jack
Frost.

"Why have you made such a mess in our beautiful library?" Aisha asked.

Four goblin arms stuck out from behind Jack Frost, each one holding a book.

"You can't take those," said Aisha. "Those are very special, and they belong to us. They must stay here at Mission Control, or discoveries everywhere will be stopped and go wrong."

"Who cares?" yelled Jack Frost. "I'm going to make all the discoveries by myself. I'll be famous! No one except me will discover anything or invent anything every again!"

There was a flash of blue lightning and a crash of thunder. Jack Frost and the goblins had completely disappeared.

Rachel and Kirsty turned to look at the Discovery Fairies.

"Without our magical notebooks, we can't keep astronauts safe, help inventors, inspire detectives or guide engineers," said Aisha. "Look what's happening to the International Space Station right now."

She tapped another screen with her wand, and the space station appeared.

"Something's wrong with it," said Rachel at once.

The space station's lights were flickering.

"The power is failing," said Aisha. "I can fix the station in the twinkling of an eye, but only if I have my magical notebook."

"Then we must find it," said Kirsty.

"Where shall we start looking?"

"Jack Frost's Castle?" Rachel suggested.

But Annie shook her head.

"I tracked the goblins with a special detective spell," she said. "Jack Frost used his magic to build a spaceship. He sent three of the goblins into space."

"He probably thought space was one place we'd never look for them," said Elsie.

"Then he was wrong," said Rachel.

She and Kirsty nodded at each other. Then they turned to look out through the glass walls of the dome. The silver rocket was still standing on the launch pad.

"We have a mission," Kirsty said. "We're going to get Aisha's magical silver notebook back and save the astronauts!"

Rachel, Kirsty and Aisha flew down to the silver rocket and climbed inside.

"Fasten your seatbelts," said Aisha. "We're going to have to go fast if we want to catch the goblins."

Up in Mission Control, the other Discovery Fairies waved to them, and then Elsie spoke into a microphone.

"Three … two … one … blast off!"

The engine roared, and then a blast of

fairy dust sent the rocket shooting into the sky. Magical sparkles surrounded them.

"We've never flown as fast as this," said Rachel.

Outside the window, the blue sky grew dark. At the same time, Rachel and Kirsty felt themselves float upwards. Their

hair fanned out around them.

"Are we still in Fairyland?" asked Kirsty, gazing at the stars outside the window.

Below them, Earth was shining blue and green.

"No, we're back in the human world," said Aisha, smiling. "Welcome to outer space."

Chapter Four
Out of this World!

Aisha tapped each girl on the head with her wand, and a silvery bubble expanded around them. Then it popped, and Rachel and Kirsty felt their feet touch the floor again.

"Now you each have your own personal gravity and oxygen," said Aisha. "We just have to stop those goblins."

Rachel and Kirsty looked out of
the window and saw a round green
spaceship spinning, looping the loop and
zigzagging among the stars.

"Why are they flying in a spaceship?"
Kirsty asked. "Are they playing at being
aliens?"

"They're heading straight towards the International Space Station," Aisha said. "If they're seen, the astronauts will think they really are aliens."

"Oh my goodness, I bet that's their plan," said Rachel with a gasp. "The goblins will make the astronauts think aliens are real. They'll write about the goblin ship and research it. All the work they do will be messed up with the wrong facts."

"We can't let the goblins spoil the work of the space station," said Aisha. "There are so many amazing true things to be discovered about space. If the research is spoiled by tricks and lies, humans will miss out on important discoveries."

"We'll stop them and we'll get your magical silver notebook back," Kirsty promised. "We just have to be quick."

Aisha pushed a lever and the rocket boosted to top speed.

"We're catching up with them," cried Rachel. "We can do it."

"If I can get close enough, I can attach a magical tow rope to their spaceship," said Aisha. "Then we can pull them back to Fairyland."

"I think we're too late," said Kirsty with a groan.

She pointed out of the window. The International Space Station was ahead of them, getting closer every second. The lights were still flickering on and off. As the fairies watched, the round green spaceship whizzed around the space station three times and then attached itself to a port.

"They're going inside," said Aisha in alarm. "We're too late."

"Don't give up," said Rachel, squeezing her hand. "If we can get on board, we can still stop them."

"But the ports are made for human-size rockets," said Kirsty. "How will we get inside?"

"Leave that to me," said Aisha. "It wasn't just human astronauts who helped to build this space station, you know."

She pressed a flashing yellow button on the control panel, and a tiny hatch rose up on top of the space station.

"A fairy port," said Rachel, delighted. "Perfect!"

Aisha docked the rocket and opened the airlock. All three fairies fluttered into the space station, and the airlock closed behind them.

"At this time of day, the astronauts will be eating in the dining module," said Aisha. "Let's see if we can find the goblins before mealtime finishes."

They flew through a long, square corridor. Wires trailed from the walls and panels of buttons bleeped and blinked. They passed the crew sleeping area and peeped into the berths, but there were no goblins to be seen. Then, above the beeps, the fairies heard a squawk of laughter.

"Goblins!" said Rachel.

They hovered and peered into the next

corridor. Three goblins were floating around the module, turning somersaults, pressing buttons and pulling wires. Each of them had a rucksack and they were all dressed up as aliens. One had a headband with googly eyes and drooping feelers. The second had three fake legs waving from a green belt around his waist, and the third had covered his head in ear stickers.

"We have to stop them," said Rachel. "They could damage the space station."

"Couldn't you send them home with your magic?" asked Kirsty, turning to Aisha.

"Yes, but not until I know which one has the magical notebook," replied the little fairy. "I have to get it back to keep the astronauts safe."

The lights flickered on and off, and a distant alarm wailed.

"I've got an idea," said Rachel. "Let's try to separate them. Maybe if we can get them into the sleeping area one by one, we can find out who has the notebook and get it back."

"We could lay a trail of something to tempt them," Kirsty suggested.

"I know the perfect thing," said Aisha with a smile.

Chapter Five
Tempting the Goblins

Aisha waved her wand, and a little green cupcake appeared in the air, bobbing up and down. She sent it floating towards the goblin with the feelers. It bumped into the back of his head and he turned around.

"Yum, cake," he said to himself.

He tried to bite the cake, but it floated away from him. With his mouth wide

open, he tried to swim through the air
towards it. But every time he got close to
it, the cake bobbed away.

"Grrr," he muttered.

Kicking his legs like a frog, he chased
the cake, getting further and further
away from the other goblins. The fairies
followed him all the way into the
sleeping area. As soon as he was inside,

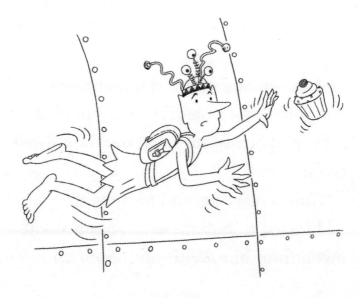

Kirsty pressed the button to close the door. The goblin turned and his mouth fell open.

"Fairies in space?" he cried. "Leave us alone!"

"Not until you give back what you've stolen," said Rachel, folding her arms. "Open your rucksack."

The goblin opened his bag. There was nothing inside. The googly eyes and droopy feelers wobbled on his head as he sniggered.

"Bad luck," he said.

"Time for you to fly home," said Aisha.

With a swish of her wand, the goblin disappeared.

"Let's try again," said Kirsty.

They flew back to the module where the other goblins were still pressing

buttons and giggling. Aisha pointed
her wand at the goblin with fake legs.
A green bubble floated from the tip. It
popped against the goblin's ear, and he
turned around.

"Ooh, bubbles," he squawked.

Aisha magicked up another bubble
and sent it floating past the goblin. He
giggled and chased it around the corner
to the sleeping area. As he popped it,
Aisha placed a bottle of bubble mixture
beside one of the berths. The goblin went

to snatch it, and Rachel closed the door.

"We won't let you fool the astronauts into thinking you're aliens," said Kirsty. "Give us the notebook you took."

The goblin unzipped his rucksack.

"Nothing," said Aisha.

She waved her wand and the goblin disappeared instantly.

"The third goblin must have the notebook," said Rachel.

"But the astronauts will finish their meal any moment now," said Aisha. "Time is running out."

The lights flickered again as the fairies zoomed back through the corridor. But when they reached the module, the third goblin had vanished.

Just then, Rachel heard a loud sniff. She peered around a corner and saw the goblin floating upside down beside a docking port. As she watched, a tear left his eye and floated upwards.

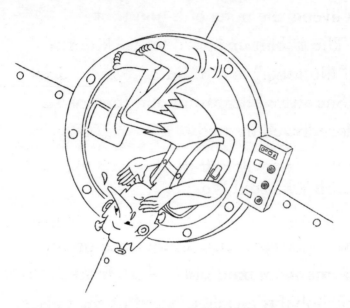

"What's the matter?" she asked.

"Leave me alone," said the goblin in a miserable voice.

Aisha and Kirsty came around the corner too.

"Maybe we can help you if you tell us what's wrong," said Kirsty.

The goblin wiped his nose on the back of his hand.

"I'm homesick," he wailed. "We used all the magic Jack Frost gave us to dress up as aliens and turn our rocket into a spaceship. Now I can't find the others and there isn't enough magic to get home. Waah!"

"Your goblin friends have gone home already," said Rachel. "You can go too. All you have to do is give back the notebook you've got in your bag."

"No way," said the goblin.

"Do the right thing," said Kirsty. "It'll feel really good."

"No, it won't," the goblin snapped. "Especially when Jack Frost finds out."

61

"Wouldn't you rather be home in Goblin Grotto than up here?" asked Rachel. "Aisha will send you home as soon as you give her back her notebook."

The goblin scowled, but he took the rucksack off his back and unzipped it.

"What about my spaceship?" he asked.

"That will have to disappear," said Aisha. "It's not nice to play tricks on humans."

"Spoilsport," the goblin huffed.

He pulled a glowing, silver notebook from his bag and then hugged it to his chest.

"I'm not giving it to you," he said. "I'm going to stay here and use it to become a famous astronaut."

"But you don't know how to use it," Aisha exclaimed.

62

"It's mine," said the goblin, sticking out his bottom lip. "And not even Jack Frost can take it away from me."

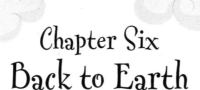

Chapter Six
Back to Earth

Aisha turned to Rachel and Kirsty.

"We have to get the notebook back somehow," she said.

"But we won't play tricks to get it," said Kirsty.

"That would make us just as naughty as him," Rachel agreed.

They turned back to the goblin and Aisha stepped forwards.

"Listen," she said in a gentle voice. "This is an amazing place. The humans have discovered so much about the world just by being up here. I can see that you love it too."

The goblin shrugged, but his eyes were shining.

"The trouble is, the space station is going to break down unless you give the notebook back," said Rachel. "It needs Aisha and her magical notebook to protect it."

"When we found you, you were crying," said Kirsty. "I think that in your heart, you miss your friends in Goblin Grotto."

The goblin let out a big sigh. Then he handed the magical notebook to Aisha. As soon as she touched it, the notebook

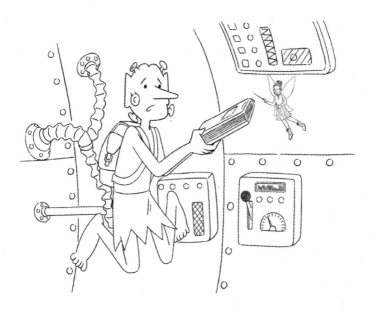

shrank to fairy size and the lights of the
space station stopped flickering.

"Thank you," whispered Aisha.

She waved her wand and the goblin
disappeared.

"We did it!" Aisha cried. "Thank you,
Rachel and Kirsty. The astronauts are
safe."

"Thank goodness," said Rachel.

"I couldn't have done it without you," Aisha said, hugging them both.

"We're so glad we could help," said Kirsty. "But right now I think we belong somewhere else."

She pointed out of a small, round window at Planet Earth.

"It's so beautiful," said Rachel. "I think it's time to go home."

"I'll send you the quick way," said Aisha, smiling. "I'll never forget our adventure. I am sure that the other Discovery Fairies will be visiting you soon."

"We'll help them however we can," Kirsty promised.

Aisha kissed them goodbye and then waved her wand. At once, the hums, beeps and crackles of the International Space Station stopped. Instead, the girls were back inside the planetarium in the Science Museum. The International Space Station filled the screen around them.

"Perhaps one day you will visit the space station in real life," the voice

boomed. "Anything is possible when you set off on a journey of discovery."

The film ended and the lights came on. The audience cheered and clapped. Rachel and Kirsty turned to each other and exchanged happy smiles. Grace, the planetarium assistant, came over to talk to them.

"Did you enjoy the show?" she asked.

The girls nodded.

"What's next?" asked Kirsty. "We can't wait to find out."

Grace laughed.

"It's great that you're so keen," she said. "Next, it's time for a rest and a snack break. After that, you should head over to the Gallery of Inventions for the second activity of the evening."

She moved away and the girls

started to make their way out of the
planetarium.

"That was so exciting," said Rachel in
a low voice. "I wonder which adventure
will come next – the science museum one
or the magical one?"

"I have a feeling that we'll soon find
out," said Kirsty. "Jack Frost still has three
of the magical notebooks."

"And we have to find them to save discoveries everywhere," said Rachel.

"Right now, I want to discover what Dad's packed in our snack boxes," said Kirsty.

Giggling, the girls hurried back to their camp. They found that Mr Tate had set out a mini feast of sausage rolls, triangle sandwiches, boiled eggs and cartons of juice.

"This looks brilliant, Dad," said Kirsty. "Thank you."

"I'm sorry I had to miss the planetarium show," said Mr Tate. "Was it exciting?"

The girls shared a knowing glance.

"It was the most realistic space journey ever," said Rachel truthfully.

"And it made me love the Science Museum even more," added Kirsty. "We can't wait to discover what's going to happen next!"

The End

**Now it's time for Kirsty and
Rachel to help ...**

Orla the Inventor Fairy

Read on for a sneak peek ...

"Wow, look, Rachel," Kirsty Tate said to
her best friend. "These cameras are more
than one hundred years old."

"Wow!" agreed Rachel Walker. "I love
photography."

The best friends were inside the Science
Museum's Gallery of Inventions, looking
at a display about cameras. They were
at the Science Museum for a very special
sleepover. Hundreds of families and
groups of friends had come to camp
inside the museum for one night. Rachel
and Kirsty had come with Mr Tate,
Kirsty's dad.

So far, it had been even more exciting than they had expected. Their visit to the planetarium had turned into a magical adventure in Fairyland. The girls had met the Discovery Fairies – Aisha the Astronaut Fairy, Orla the Inventor Fairy, Annie the Detective Fairy and Elsie the Engineer Fairy. They were all very worried because Jack Frost had broken into Mission Control and stolen their magical notebooks.

"I can't wait to find out what the next activity will be," said Rachel.

"Me too," said Kirsty. "But I keep thinking about the Discovery Fairies. Without their magical notebooks, they can't help to inspire people who make amazing discoveries or invent things like these cameras."

"We've already helped them to get one of the notebooks back," said Rachel. "I'm sure that soon we'll get the chance to help find the others."

Just then, an elderly man in a suit clapped his hands to get everyone's attention. The boys, girls and parents gathered around him.

"Welcome to the Gallery of Inventions," he said. "My name is Professor Aldous Fidget. From the wheel to the computer, the world has been made a better place by imaginative inventors who had a dream and made it come true. So, what's your dream?"

"A flying car," shouted out a little girl.

"A time machine!" called a little boy.

"A self-watering flowerpot," said another girl.

"All excellent ideas," said Professor

Fidget, clapping his hands. "We have a great activity for you. We would like you to become inventors for the evening. On the tables in the middle of the gallery are all sorts of inspiring things. There are also tablets for you to work on. We can't wait to see what you make."

Read **Orla the Inventor Fairy** to find out what adventures are in store for Kirsty and Rachel!

Calling all parents, carers and teachers!
The Rainbow Magic fairies are here to help
your child enter the magical world of reading.
Whatever reading stage they are at, there's
a Rainbow Magic book for everyone!
Here is Lydia the Reading Fairy's guide to
supporting your child's journey at all levels.

(1)

Starting Out
Our Rainbow Magic Beginner Readers are perfect for first-time readers who are just beginning to develop reading skills and confidence. Approved by teachers, they contain a full range of educational levelling, as well as lively full-colour illustrations.

(2)

Developing Readers
Rainbow Magic Early Readers contain longer stories and wider vocabulary for building stamina and growing confidence. These are adaptations of our most popular Rainbow Magic stories, specially developed for younger readers in conjunction with an Early Years reading consultant, with full-colour illustrations.

(3)

Going Solo
The Rainbow Magic chapter books – a mixture of series and one-off specials – contain accessible writing to encourage your child to venture into reading independently. These highly collectible and much-loved magical stories inspire a love of reading to last a lifetime.

www.rainbowmagicbooks.co.uk

"Rainbow Magic got my daughter reading chapter books. Great sparkly covers, cute fairies and traditional stories full of magic that she found impossible to put down" – Mother of Edie (6 years)

"Florence LOVES the Rainbow Magic books. She really enjoys reading now" – Mother of Florence (6 years)

The Rainbow Magic Reading Challenge

Well done, fairy friend – you have completed the book!
This book was worth 5 points.

See how far you have climbed on the
Reading Rainbow opposite.

The more books you read, the more points you will get,
and the closer you will be to becoming a Fairy Princess!

How to get your Reading Rainbow
1. Cut out the coin below
2. Go to the Rainbow Magic website
3. Download and print out your poster
4. Add your coin and climb up the Reading Rainbow!

There's all this and lots more at
www.rainbowmagicbooks.co.uk

You'll find activities, competitions, stories, a special
newsletter and complete profiles of all the
Rainbow Magic fairies. Find a fairy with your name!